Young Princesses
AROUND THE WORLD

Cleopatra and the King's Enemies

Based on a True Story of Cleopatra in Egypt

BY JOAN HOLUB • ILLUSTRATED BY NONNA ALESHINA

READY-TO-READ • ALADDIN
NEW YORK   LONDON   TORONTO   SYDNEY

This book is a work of historical fiction based on the author's careful research of historical facts and events. Dialogue and many events are the product of the author's imagination, and any resemblance to actual events or persons, living or dead, is entirely coincidental.

ALADDIN PAPERBACKS
An imprint of Simon & Schuster Children's Publishing Division
1230 Avenue of the Americas, New York, NY 10020
Text copyright © 2007 by Joan Holub
Illustrations copyright © 2007 by PiArt & Design Agency
READY-TO-READ, ALADDIN PAPERBACKS, and related logo
are registered trademarks of Simon & Schuster, Inc.
Also available in an Aladdin library edition.
Designed by Karin Paprocki
The text of this book was set in Century Oldstyle BT.
Manufactured in the United States of America
First Aladdin Paperbacks edition March 2007
2 4 6 8 10 9 7 5 3 1
Library of Congress Cataloging-in-Publication Data
Holub, Joan.
Cleopatra and the king's enemies : a true story of Cleopatra in Egypt /
by Joan Holub ; illustrated by Nonna Aleshina.—1st ed.
p. cm.—(Ready-to-read) (Young princesses around the world ; #2)
ISBN-13: 978-0-689-87196-2   ISBN-10: 0-689-87196-1 (lib. bdg.)
ISBN-13: 978-0-689-87194-8   ISBN-10: 0-689-87194-5 (pbk.)
1. Cleopatra, Queen of Egypt, d. 30 B.C.—Juvenile literature.
2. Queens—Egypt—Biography—Juvenile literature. I. Aleshina, Nonna., ill.
II. Title. III. Series: Holub, Joan. Young princesses around the world ; #2.
DT92.7.H65 2007   932' .021092—dc22   2006010104

For Paula Tacha

4

CHAPTER 1

Cleopatra and the King's Enemies

Nine-year-old Princess Cleopatra frowned at her reflection in the waters of the fountain one morning.

"My nose is too big," she said.

Cleopatra's older sisters, Tryphaena and Berenice, smiled.

The three princesses were in the royal palace in Alexandria, Egypt. They were getting ready for a feast that night. The feast was to honor their father, the king of Egypt.

Tryphaena looked into her mirror. She combed her long, black hair. There was a cone of wax on top of her head. The wax would melt during the warm evening and smell of perfume.

"That's true. You will never be as beautiful as I," she told Cleopatra.

Berenice giggled. "Nor I. Even makeup cannot make your face beautiful!"

Cleopatra jumped up, her sandals tapping the marble floor.

"I would rather be smart than pretty," she told her sisters. But deep inside, she wasn't so sure.

The sound of her sisters' mean laughter followed Cleopatra down the hall. As she passed three servants, they bowed and then continued working.

"My feet hurt," one of them said.

"I know a place where we can hide and rest for a while," said another.

"Let's go. Why should we work hard for a false king?" said the third.

The servants spoke in the Egyptian language, not knowing that Cleopatra understood them. Everyone else in Cleopatra's family spoke only Greek. With her teacher's help, Cleopatra had learned six languages. This made it easy for her to overhear secrets.

Cleopatra met her teacher in the library.

"Why are you here?" he asked in surprise. "Your lessons are not until tomorrow."

"I had to get away from my horrible sisters," said Cleopatra.

Her teacher unrolled a large sheet of papyrus with writing on it. "This will take your mind off of them."

Cleopatra read the story of her favorite hero aloud: " 'A brave Greek named Alexander the Great conquered Egypt over two hundred and fifty years ago. Ever since then, a Greek family has ruled Egypt.'

"That is *my* family," Cleopatra said proudly.

ALEXANDRIA

MEDITERRANEAN SEA

CAIRO

NILE RIVER

EGYPT

RED SEA

11

Suddenly they heard shouting outside in the garden. Cleopatra looked out the window. Guards were leading an angry man away.

"Death to King Auletes!" the man shouted.

Cleopatra was worried. "Why do the Egyptians dislike my father so much?"

"Because he is the king of Egypt," said her teacher. "Yet he is not Egyptian."

"No. We are Greek," said Cleopatra. "But perhaps even a Greek king could make the Egyptian people happy if he listened to what they want."

"Too bad your father does not understand their Egyptian words as you do, Princess," said her teacher.

That gave Cleopatra an idea!

CHAPTER 2

Cleopatra the Spy

Back in her room Cleopatra took off her linen gown and veil. She put on one of her servant's plain dresses.

"I am going to the market," Cleopatra told her servant.

The servant gasped. "But the king does not want you and the other princesses to leave the palace! Someone may try to harm you."

Cleopatra planned to
help her father by listening to the
Egyptians in the market. But she did not
want her servant to know about her plan.

"No one will recognize me in your dress," said Cleopatra. "I will return before father's feast begins."

"Be careful!" the servant begged.

But Cleopatra was already on her way. She slipped out of the royal garden and beyond the palace walls.

Soon she was in the busy outdoor
market on the shores of Alexandria.
It was crowded with people buying and
selling.

"Olives! Plums! Fig cakes!" called
one shopkeeper.

"Bread and cheese!" called another.

Cleopatra stopped at a shop that sold
bread, and began listening carefully.

A woman at the bread shop threw down a loaf of bread in disgust. "This bread is moldy!" she complained.

The shopkeeper shrugged. "The Nile River gives Egypt a good wheat harvest each year, but the king sells our wheat to the Romans to feed their soldiers. I must make do with what I have."

"The Romans want more than our wheat," said the woman. "They want to add Egypt to their Roman Empire!"

The shopkeeper nodded. "And they may do just that. The king borrowed money from them and raised our taxes to pay them back. We are poor. But if we do not repay the Romans, their armies will come."

Taxes had made her father even more enemies, thought Cleopatra.

"Rome is like a cat waiting to pounce on a mouse. And Egypt is the mouse!" someone else added.

"This mess is the king's fault. I will make him sorry he ever befriended the Romans," said a man dressed in green robes.

Cleopatra could not see the man's face. She leaned closer.

"Move along, peasant!" the bread shopkeeper shouted at her. He gave her a shove. Cleopatra fell.

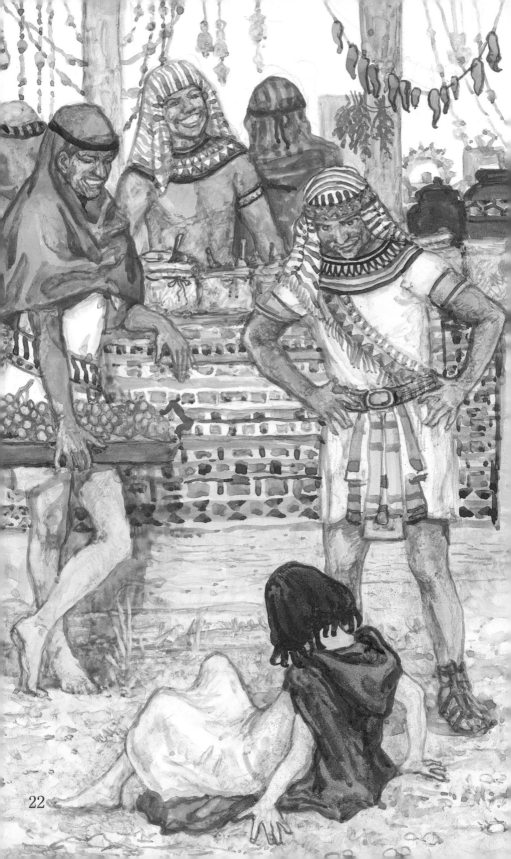

"How dare you!" Cleopatra said.

The shopkeeper laughed. "This peasant girl with the big nose acts like she's a princess!"

People nearby laughed too. Cleopatra looked around, worried. If anyone discovered she *was* a princess, there would be trouble.

Cleopatra wanted to get a better look at the face of the man in the green robes, but he was gone. The sun was setting over the nearby sea. It was almost time for her father's feast to begin! Cleopatra hurried home.

3

Cleopatra Saves the King

Back at the palace Cleopatra quickly changed into her linen dress and purple veil.

On her way to the feast hall, she met her father. She had disobeyed his rules by leaving the palace. She did not dare tell him that she had gone to the market.

But she had to warn him.

"I believe there may be enemies among our guests," she told him. "Please be careful tonight."

"Do not worry. The palace guards will take care of any enemies. Come along. Everyone is waiting for us," he said.

Cleopatra and the king entered the feast hall. Tryphaena and Berenice were already there.

The room was filled with guests, servants, dancers, and musicians.

Cleopatra heard Latin, Syrian, Egyptian, Greek, Nubian, and Hebrew being spoken. She understood all of these languages.

"The king is getting fat," a man in green robes said as Cleopatra and her father passed.

"And his daughter Cleopatra is too skinny," said his friend.

The two men had been speaking in Egyptian, so the king did not understand them. But Cleopatra did. She frowned.

Are those the same men I overheard in the market? she wondered.

The king went to sit on his throne.

"May we hear a song?" the man in green asked the king, speaking in Greek.

Cleopatra's father smiled. He was pleased to know that someone wanted to hear him play the flute.

But Cleopatra did not trust the man.

"Father!" she whispered. "Those men are not our friends. They were making fun of us."

The king did not listen to her. Instead he began to play a tune.

Cleopatra moved closer to the man in green and his friend so she could hear them over the music.

The men were not worried about the princess being nearby. They spoke to each other in Egyptian, thinking she would not understand them.

"I have poisoned the king's wine," said the man in green robes.

"Once he is dead, we will crown a true Egyptian king," said his friend.

They grinned.

Suddenly the king's music stopped.

"Playing the flute has made me thirsty," Cleopatra heard her father say. He picked up his wineglass.

Cleopatra ran toward him. Dancers and guests were in her way. Would she reach her father in time?

"Wait!" shouted Cleopatra. She knocked the wineglass from the king's hand.

Everyone in the banquet hall gasped. Her father frowned at her.

"Your wine was poisoned," Cleopatra explained quickly. She pointed at her father's two enemies. "And *they* did it."

"Bring those men here!" the king shouted to his guards.

The men were brought to stand before the king.

"Your daughter has made a mistake," the one in green said. He spoke in Greek so that the king could understand him. He looked brave.

The other man looked scared.

"Do not worry," the one in green told his friend in Egyptian. "The skinny princess didn't understand our Egyptian words earlier. She is just guessing."

"You are wrong," Cleopatra replied. "I understood every word you said. And I am *not* skinny!"

The two men gasped in surprise.

"Put them in jail!" shouted her father.

The men were led away in chains.

Cleopatra saw her sisters sitting nearby. They looked amazed. *Maybe being smart really* is *more important than being beautiful*, she thought.

"Thank you for saving my life," the king told Cleopatra.

She smiled. She had saved her father from danger that night.

But there was more trouble brewing.

CHAPTER

The Princesses' Plot

One month later Cleopatra and her two sisters waved good-bye to the king. He was going to sail across the Mediterranean Sea to Rome.

"The Egyptian people want a different king," said Tryphaena, after the king's ship had set sail. "Our father plans to ask the Roman Army to help him keep his throne."

"I hope he is successful," said Cleopatra.

"He won't be," said Tryphaena. "He will only make the Romans think Egypt is weak and easily conquered. Father is a fool and a bad ruler. I have decided to take over as queen in his place."

Cleopatra gasped. "You cannot!"

"Who is going to stop me?" asked Tryphaena.

"Why should you be queen? Why not me?" whined Berenice.

Cleopatra jumped up. "Stop! Both of you just want to be rich and powerful. Egypt needs a wise ruler who will lead it well and take care of its people."

"I suppose you think *you* should be queen someday?" asked Tryphaena in between laughs.

"That is for father to decide," Cleopatra replied. "He is the king."

"Just imagine your plain face on a coin as queen! It would scare people," said Berenice.

Cleopatra frowned at her.

She knew her father was not always a wise ruler. But he was her father and the king. She would be loyal to him no matter what.

Cleopatra ran to her room and pulled out her writing box. Quickly she wrote a note on a sheet of papyrus.

Dearest Father,

Beware. Tryphaena and Berenice are plotting to betray you.

Please return soon.

—Princess Cleopatra

She rolled the papyrus up tightly. "Send this message to my father," she whispered to a trusted servant.

Some people in Egypt thought Berenice would be a good ruler. They killed Tryphaena a few months later, and Berenice became the queen. Two years after that, the king returned from Rome.

"Bring Berenice to me!" he shouted as he entered the palace.

Cleopatra and her teacher watched from the balcony as Berenice was

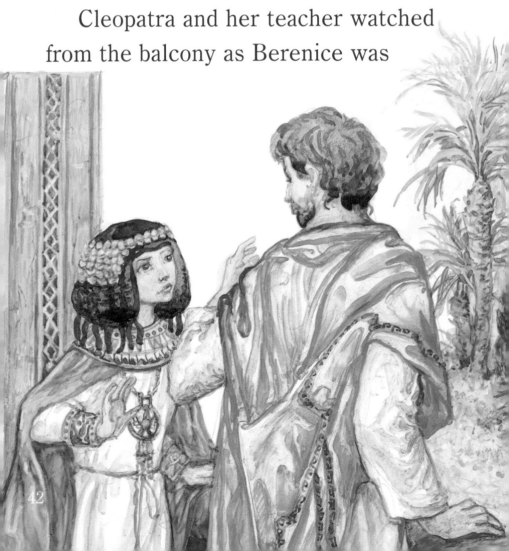

brought before the king. Minutes later she was dragged from the palace in chains.

"The king is angry," said Cleopatra. "What will he do to her?"

"Death is the punishment for disloyalty to the king," said her teacher. "She will be executed."

"How awful!" said Cleopatra.

"Where is Cleopatra?" her father shouted.

"Oh, no!" said Cleopatra. Was her father afraid she might betray him someday as her sisters had? Would she be executed too?

She slowly walked downstairs to stand before him.

The king put a hand on her shoulder. Then he smiled.

"You are wise and loyal, Princess Cleopatra," he told her. "And you will be rewarded. I promise that someday *you* will be queen of Egypt."

5

Queen Cleopatra

Cleopatra was just eighteen years old when she became queen of Egypt.

Many other countries wanted to rule Egypt and control its rich farmlands along the Nile River. But Cleopatra outsmarted these enemies.

Cleopatra made mistakes and was not perfect. But her face did wind up on a beautiful coin, and she became the most famous queen of Egypt ever.

This approximate time line lists important events in Cleopatra's life:

80 B.C.	Cleopatra's father, Auletes (Ptolemy XII), becomes king of Egypt.
69 B.C.	Cleopatra VII is born in Alexandria, the capital of Egypt. She is the seventh girl named Cleopatra in the history of her family.
66 B.C.	Her mother dies.
58 B.C.	Her sisters plot to overthrow their father, the king.
51 B.C.	Cleopatra's father dies, and she becomes queen of Egypt at age eighteen. Her ten-year-old brother becomes co-ruler.
49 B.C.	Cleopatra is overthrown and flees to Syria.
48 B.C.	A Roman leader named Julius Caesar (SEE-zer) comes to Egypt. Cleopatra sneaks back into Egypt hidden in a large rolled carpet. Caesar makes her queen again. Her brother is killed.
47 B.C.	Cleopatra and Caesar take a sailing trip on the Nile River. She gives birth to her first son.
46 B.C.	The Romans are angry that Caesar allows her to live in his Roman palace.
44 B.C.	Caesar is murdered by Roman senators on March 15. Cleopatra returns to Egypt.
41 B.C.	She falls in love with Marc Antony, a Roman leader. Some historians believe they married five years later.
32 B.C.	Rome declares war against Cleopatra and Antony.
31 B.C.	She and Antony lose a great sea battle, and soon lose the war.
30 B.C.	Cleopatra does not want the Romans to capture her alive. She lets a poisonous snake called an asp bite her. She dies at age thirty-nine.